Text and illustration copyright © Siphano 1998

First American publication 1998 by
The Millbrook Press, Inc.
2 Old New Milford Road
Brookfield, Connecticut 06804

Morichon, David.
    Pollution? no problem! / David Morichon. – 1st American ed.
        p.   cm.
    Summary: When Albert's new invention begins to seep goo, he and
his friend Henry discover that getting rid of the pollution is a big problem.
    ISBN 0-7613-1260-9 (lib. bdg.).
    [1. Pollution – Fiction.   2. Environmental protection – Fiction.]
I. Title.
PZ7.M826745Po   1998
[E]–dc21   98-5690
                                                                 CIP
Color separation: Atelier 6, Montpellier, France
Printed in Italy by Grafiche AZ, Verona
5   4   3   2   1

David Morichon

POLLUTION?
NO PROBLEM!

The Millbrook Press
Brookfield, Connecticut

Albert asked his friend Henry to help him with his new invention.
The two had worked hard all morning. They had measured and
hammered and welded. Just a few more bolts and the machine
would be ready.

Henry was tired of working and wanted to play, but Albert
couldn't wait to finish the machine. They stopped work to eat
their lunch in the shade of a tree. Albert spoke of the wonderful
things his new machine would make.

Plastic bottles,
garbage cans,
beach balls,
batteries, tires...
Their life would be
so much easier.

But just a moment!
Albert spotted some
seeping goo. What could
it be?

"Pollution?

No problem!

I can handle it.

I will build a wheelbarrow
and I will take the pollution
and bury it at the very edge of the forest."

Albert dug a hole and hid the pollution
deep in the ground. He covered up the hole...
and he even planted a flower on top.

PERFECT!

"Pollution?

No problem!

But look,
the flower is wilting...

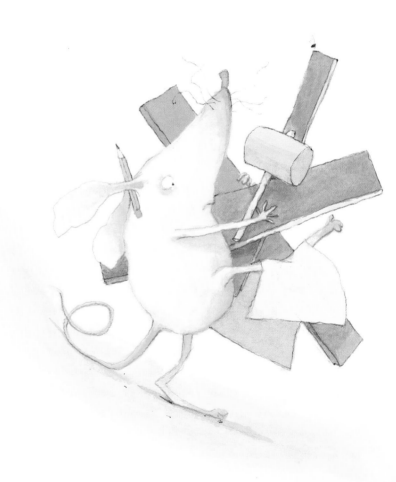

I will build...   **...a submarine on wheels...**

...and I will take the pollution
far, far away...

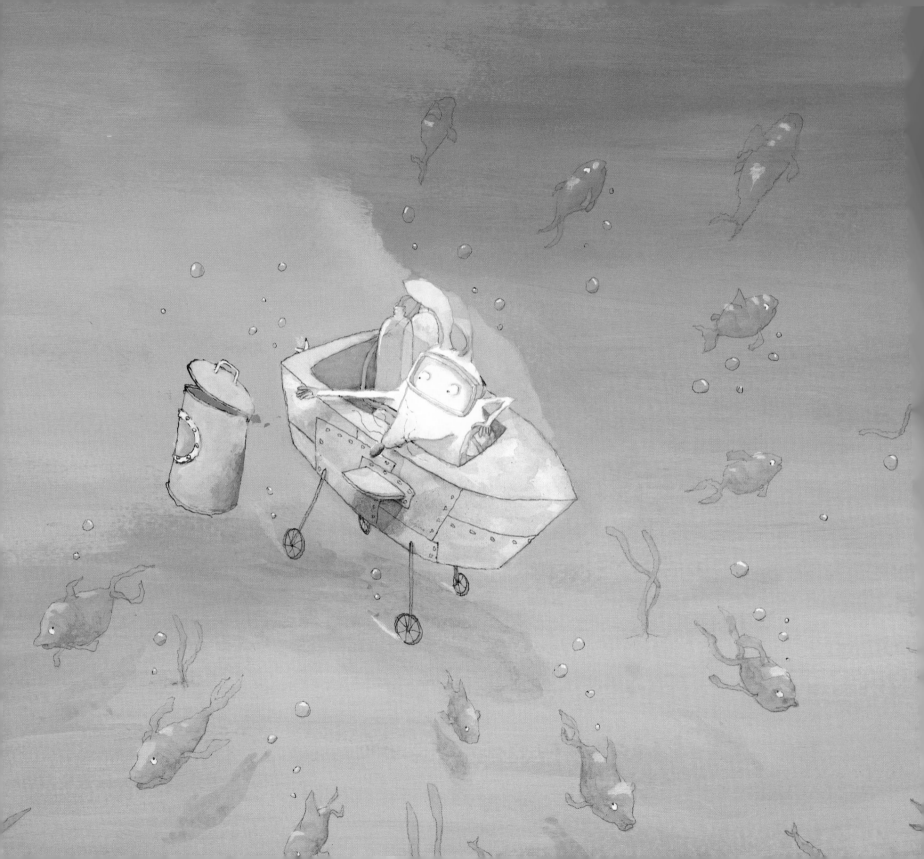

...and dump it on the bottom of the ocean."

But wait!
The pollution traveled quicker than Albert.
It is back in the forest, under the trees...

The forest is sick and everyone is running away.

"Pollution?

No problem!"

shouted Albert.

"I will build a rocket
and I will carry the pollution...

...far, far, far, far away...

...and I will dump it on the moon.

It's finished! Pollution will never come back."
Albert is very pleased with himself. But wait!
What's that overhead?
What are those clouds coming closer...

and closer...   ...and closer?

Oh, no! It's raining!
It's raining gooey, purple pollution.

Pollution is everywhere.

It is on the trees.
It is on the ground.
It is on Albert.

Albert wakes up. He and Henry had fallen asleep. The machine was still there.

"I'm tired of helping you work on the machine," said Henry. "Our friends are waiting for us to play."

"NO PROBLEM!" said Albert happily. "Let's forget about finishing the machine."

And off they went to play in the sunshine.